This book belongs to

....

I celebrated World Book Day 2018
with this brilliant gift from my local
Bookseller and Puffin Books.

D0532601

CELEBRATE STORIES. LOVE READING.

This book has been specially written and published to celebrate **World Book Day**. We are a charity who offers every child and young person the opportunity to read and love books by offering you the chance to have a book of your own. To find out more, as well as oodles of fun activities and reading recommendations to continue your reading journey, visit **worldbookday.com**

World Book Day in the UK and Ireland is made possible by generous sponsorship from National Book Tokens, participating publishers, booksellers, authors and illustrators. The £1 book tokens are a gift from your local Bookseller.

World Book Day works in partnership with a number of charities, all of whom are working to encourage a love of reading for pleasure.

The National Literacy Trust is an independent charity that encourages children to enjoy reading. Just 10 minutes of reading every day can make a big difference to how well you do at school and to how successful you could be in life. **literacytrust.org.uk**

The Reading Agency inspires people of all ages and backgrounds to read for pleasure and empowerment. They run the Summer Reading Challenge in partnership with libraries, as well as supporting reading groups in schools and libraries all year round. Find out more and join your local library. **summerreadingchallenge.org.uk**

World Book Day also facilitates fundraising for:

Book Aid International, an international book donation and library development charity. Every year, they provide one million books to libraries and schools in communities where children would otherwise have little or no opportunity to read. **bookaid.org.uk**

Read for Good, who motivate children in schools to read for fun through its sponsored read, which thousands of schools run on World Book Day and throughout the year. The money raised provides new books and resident storytellers in all of the UK's children's hospitals. **readforgood.org**

*€1.50 in Ireland

BRAIN FREEZE

TOM FLETCHER

Illustrations by Shane Devries

PUFFIN

PUFFIN BOOKS

UK | USA | Canada | Ireland | Australia
India | New Zealand | South Africa

Puffin Books is part of the Penguin Random House group of companies
whose addresses can be found at global.penguinrandomhouse.com.

www.penguin.co.uk www.puffin.co.uk www.ladybird.co.uk

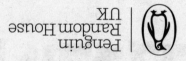

First published 2018

001

Set in Baskerville MT Std
Text design by Mandy Norman
Printed in Great Britain by Clays Ltd, St Ives plc

A CIP catalogue record for this book is available from the British Library

ISBN: 978-0-241-32372-4

All correspondence to:
Puffin Books
Penguin Random House Children's
80 Strand, London WC2R 0RL

For Nan and Grandad –
thanks for always having choc ices in the freezer

CHAPTER ONE
THE END

The End.

OK, I know that's not how stories usually start, but this is my story about time travel, and the thing about time travel is that not everything happens in the right order. The end can be at the beginning, the middle can be at the end, and the beginning . . . well, sometimes that just happens randomly in the second paragraph.

'Izzy, close your mouth when you're eating!' Mum nagged at me from across the dinner table as a lump of tasteless broccoli slopped out of my open mouth.

'Yuck!' I winced.
'It tastes like tree poop!'

'I know you don't like it, Iz, but if you want ice cream for pudding, then you have to eat your greens,' Dad said in his best negotiating voice.

The thing is, I knew I would get ice cream for pudding whether I ate my greens or not.

It was non-negotiable.

You see, it was like this: once a day, no matter what, I ate ice cream. I'm not talking about that fancy-pants Italian gelato stuff that everyone bangs on about, and not that non-dairy, sugar-free, zero-calorie slush either. I'm talking about good old-fashioned swirly vanilla ice cream in a cone with a chocolatey Flake shoved in the top. If it comes with sprinkles and fudge sauce too, then that's even better.

That's the kind of ice cream I ate every day. Without fail. It was a promise I'd made to myself last year.

Why?

Well, I guess that takes me nicely to the next part of my story.

My grandpa was an ice-cream man.

Yep – Gramps had one of those big ice-cream vans. I know, it's cool, isn't it? His was as blue as the sky, and it matched his kind, twinkly eyes perfectly. For years and years Gramps had driven around our village with that magical music chiming out of the speakers on top.

My earliest memory is of being in his van on a hot summer's day, sitting on the cold freezer, enjoying an ice cream while Gramps served the queue of kids waiting outside. He made serving ice cream look like a dance. He'd flip the cone out of the box and roll it up his arm like a basketball before spinning it round on the tip of his finger. Then he'd flip down the handle on the ice-cream machine and, while the cone was still spinning, he'd pour out the twirliest, twistiest, yummiest ice cream, and everyone in the queue would applaud.

He'd serve ice cream all day until the little flashing light on the freezer turned from green to red – **full to empty!** When that happened, he'd sigh and say, 'All gone for today!' and we'd drive home.

That was a long time ago, though, before Gramps fell ill – too ill to work any more. I remember the day Dad parked the ice-cream van in our garage at the bottom of the garden, and the way a little teardrop fell from Gramps's eye as the engine cut out for the last time.

It broke Gramps's heart to see his pride and joy sitting in the shadows between the lawnmower and the ladder, gathering dust. He asked me about it every time I went to visit him in hospital. I remember walking into his room for the first time with a big blue balloon to cheer him up. 'Blue, *just like my van*,' he'd said, beaming. Every day after that, I would walk straight there after school, arriving as Nurse Rita wheeled in his dinner tray.

'What's for pudding, Izzy?' he'd always say, propping himself up on the pillow.

Ice cream! I would cheer, spotting two little tubs of delicious, swirly ice cream. Nurse Rita would always sneak an extra one on to Gramps's dinner tray for me each night. It must have been against hospital regulations, as she would scratch her head and act surprised, saying something like 'How on earth did that get there?' or 'I don't know where that came from!'

Even though Gramps was poorly, those hospital visits were the best. I'd sit on the end of his hospital bed, eating ice cream and listening to his stories – and he always told **THE BEST** stories. They were all about the places he'd been and the things he'd seen. There was the story about the time he'd climbed a tree to avoid being eaten by a hungry **T. Rex** and had to distract it by feeding it Fab lollies while he slid down its scaly tail to escape. Or the one about the time he'd accidentally reversed the ice-cream van into a pyramid in ancient Egypt and had to give **Tutankhamun** a free 99 Flake to say sorry.

I knew his stories were all made up and silly, but they were great fun, and his twinkly blue eyes twinkled even more when he told them, and that made me happy.

There was only one night I didn't get to see him when he was in the hospital.

The night of my stupid school orchestra concert.

I played the cymbals – you know, the two ridiculous big metal plates you smash together. I only had to remember to smash them together once, at the end of 'Bare Necessities', but, as the eyes of a hundred proud parents watched us, all I could think about was poor Gramps eating his ice cream alone. I was so distracted that I missed the cue and forgot to smash the cymbals anyway.

By the time the concert was finished, visiting hours at the hospital were over.

'Can't we pop in quickly?' I'd pleaded. 'Just for a little ice cream?'

'Not tonight, Iz,' Mum had said.

'Just a single scoop?'

'You'll see Gramps tomorrow.'

But that was the night we got the call.

I wouldn't be seeing Gramps tomorrow. Or the next day.

Gramps had died.

From that night on I promised myself I would eat ice cream every single day. No matter what.

For Gramps.

CHAPTER TWO
NO ICE CREAM

'Izzy . . .' said Dad, coming out of the kitchen as I forced down my last piece of broccoli. 'I'm sorry, but it looks like there's no ice cream tonight.'

'**What?!**' I gasped.

'I'm sorry, Iz – it's the freezer. It's packed up and everything's melted!' Dad explained. He sounded nervous, and I could tell he knew that this was going to go down about as well as Mum's broccoli.

'**B-but . . . but . . .**' I stuttered as

he stepped out of the way, revealing the stupid broken freezer with its stupid door wide open and its should-be-frozen contents oozing on to the floor. I was trying hard to think of a way to unmelt the puddle of creamy goodness that was forming at the foot of the busted freezer, but then I remembered that I'm a ten-year-old girl, not a frozen food scientist!

'It's still ice cream – it can be saved!' I cried, lunging for the cutlery drawer and snatching a spoon before diving head first towards the river of vanilla flowing through the cracks of the kitchen tiles.

'Stop her, Peter!' Mum screeched, and Dad leapt towards me with his arms outstretched.

There was no time for spoons.

I needed ice cream.

'ISABELLE!
Do NOT lick the floor!'

Mum shouted as I began slurping up as much melted ice cream as I could before Dad hoisted me in the air.

'But . . . I . . . must . . . have . . . ice . . . cream!' I struggled. 'For . . . Gramps!'

Silence.

Dad put me down gently, and Mum came over with that awful look of worry on her face. Actually, she'd had that look on her face every day since Gramps . . . well, you know . . . but right then, at that moment, it was even *more* that look.

'Iz, you don't have to have ice cream *every* night,' Mum said, wiping the melted ice cream off my chin.

'But what if I forget him?' I said.

Mum looked at Dad.

Dad looked at his watch.

They both sighed.

'Well, the corner shop might still be open. If we hurry, we might just make it . . . Izzy?'

I was already out of the front door.

'Come on!' I said, begging Dad to walk faster as I ran down the hill from our house towards the corner shop.

'Blimey, Izzy! I'm going as fast as I can!' Dad puffed, running after me and trying not to stumble.

The funny thing about the corner shop in our village was that it wasn't actually on the corner. It was in the middle of the street, between a post office and a house, but 'middle shop' didn't sound right, so everyone called it the corner shop anyway.

The sun was beginning to set, its light slowly fading. The street lamps suddenly flicked on and my heart sank. I could see the corner shop and the sign hanging behind the glass door.

CLOSED!

It was over. That night was going to be the first ice-cream-less night.

'Never mind, Iz,' Dad said, rubbing my back as we trudged home. 'There was always going to be one night when you couldn't have ice cream.'

I went straight to bed with an empty stomach and a head full of thoughts.

Actually, it was full of only one thought – Gramps.

I thought about his stories. I thought about his laugh. I thought about his twinkling blue eyes . . . or were they green? No, blue, definitely blue.

My heart skipped a beat. All of a sudden I couldn't remember what colour his eyes were. I mean, I knew they were blue, just like his ice-cream van, but I couldn't see them as clearly as usual in my mind. It was like I was starting to forget!

I sprang out of bed in an instant. I needed to see something. Something that would put the colour back into my memories of Gramps's eyes.

I needed to see his van!

Creeping out of the house was easy enough. Dad snored so loudly it was like Darth Vader was sleeping in the next room, and Mum wore earplugs to block out the noise. With them both fast asleep, I slipped into my clothes from earlier and walked briskly down to the kitchen. I paused at the back door and checked that no one was watching. I knew there wasn't anybody, but when you're up to no good in the middle of the night it's always wise to check over your shoulder.

Dad suddenly let out a loud pig-like snort

from upstairs and I quickly used it to drown out the sound of me cracking the back door open.

I was outside. So far, so good!

It was a warm summer's night. There were insects buzzing around the bird feeder beneath the walnut tree, and my wooden swing, which hung from its thickest branch, swung gently in the breeze.

A bat suddenly flitted past, snatching a moth mid-flight right in front of my face at the exact same moment that the village clock chimed midnight.

The bat-and-bell combo scared me so much that a little yelp blurted out of my mouth!

Izzy, be quiet, you twerp! I thought to myself. *You'll wake someone up.*

I glanced at Mum and Dad's bedroom window, which overlooked the garden. It was a hot night and the window was open, which was meant to let some air in but seemed mostly to let Dad's snores out.

Dad's snores . . . They'd stopped!

You're a goner! I thought. *You're going to be caught in the garden in the middle of the night. You're such a —*

Then my thought was interrupted by the sound of the loo flushing, and a few minutes later Dad's snores returned.

Phew!

I took a breath and kept moving towards the garage at the end of the garden. All I could think of were Gramps's eyes. I was desperately trying to picture exactly what shade of blue they were, but I kept seeing swimming-pool blue, or light-sabre blue, or Cookie Monster blue. Gramps's eyes weren't any of *those* blues.

I *had* to see his ice-cream van. I had to colour in my memory.

I stepped on the pebbled slabs that were dotted across the lawn like stepping stones. I could see the garage. I was halfway there when . . .

SPLOSHHHHHHH!

The sprinkler system sprang into life, showering the grass – and me – with water that was even colder than ice cream!

I ran through it, heading for the largest plant pot at the edge of the lawn. I lifted it and revealed the key for the garage doors. I ran over, unlocked the doors and pulled them open before jumping inside, away from the cold spray of the sprinkler.

I was out of breath and everything was

so quiet all of a sudden that I could hear my heartbeat pounding in my ears. I felt like a criminal about to steal a car.

It's your own garage! I told myself.

Yeah, you're right, I thought back.

Of course I am, I agreed.

I closed the doors behind me and flicked the light on. The harsh fluorescent tubes blinded me for a moment, but my eyes quickly adjusted, and there it was – Gramps's glorious ice-cream van, covered in dust.

I reached out my hand and slid my palm over its curved surface. I brushed through the dull dust, painting a road of fresh, shiny blue in the cool metal.

The blue I was looking for!

I took it in, then closed my eyes and thought of Gramps. **It had worked!** His eyes were all blue and twinkly again in my memory.

I smiled. I'd got what I came for.

I was about to leave when I spotted something that stopped me in my tracks.

The door to the ice-cream van.

It was open.

CHAPTER THREE
ICE CREAM
AFTER ALL

How could the door be open?

'Hello?' I called, but it came out as more of a squeak. Not because I was scared. I was just . . . erm, OK, well, maybe I was a little scared!

There was no answer. I shrugged it off and started to leave, but something made me stop as my hand was about to switch the light off.

My tummy **rumbled**!

Now, I'm not sure if all tummies speak the same language. I'm not saying that I would be able to understand what *your* tummy was saying if it rumbled at me, but I could certainly tell what *mine* was saying.

Ice cream!

I placed my hand on my tummy. 'I'm sorry, not tonight,' I said.

I raised my hand once more to turn off the light when . . .

ICE CREAM! my tummy moaned

again.

I was about to ignore it, but then my brain decided to chip in on the conversation.

What about the van? Brain said.

'What about it?' I replied.

There could be ice cream in it!

Yes, great idea, Brain! Tummy chimed.

'Of course there won't be!' I said.

But how can you be sure? asked Brain.

Worth a look if you ask me, added Tummy.

I sighed and turned to look at the suspicious open door.

Let's vote! chimed Brain. *All those in favour of checking inside Gramps's van for leftover ice cream say,* **'Aye!'**

Aye! rumbled Tummy.

Aye! voted Brain.

'Well, looks like I'm outvoted!' I huffed.

I crept up to the open door on the driver's side and quickly peered inside. There was no one there.

That's when I spotted them. The keys!

The keys to the ice-cream van were dangling from the ignition, swinging slightly as though someone had just switched the engine off.

Goosebumps popped up all down my arms. This was getting a little freaky! I wanted to run back to the house, but I was stopped by something.

Something **amazing**.

Something **not possible**.

A little light was blinking at the back of the van. It was the light on the ice-cream machine . . . and it was green.

The ice-cream machine was full!

Told you so, said Brain.

'Not now – I'm thinking!' I told it firmly.

There's ice cream to be eaten! rumbled Tummy.

I couldn't tell you exactly what happened next. They say that sharks can smell a drop of blood in the ocean from three miles away. Well, it was as if I was a shark – and vanilla ice cream was my prey. Before I knew it I had jumped over the driver's seat, laid my head down underneath the pump of the ice-cream machine and pulled the handle!

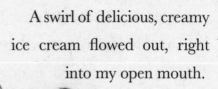

A swirl of delicious, creamy
ice cream flowed out, right
into my open mouth.
I ate.
And ate.
And ate.

Nom nom nom.

Gobble gobble
gobble.

Yum yum yum.

I paused for a second and took a breath. It was all just too overwhelming. I was so full of my favourite delicious ice cream. I couldn't possible eat any mo—

NOM NOM NOM NOM NOM!!!!!!!

Then it hit me.

'Oh gosh!' I said.

What is it? asked my very full tummy.

'It's . . . B-Brain . . .' I stuttered.

Brain? What's up? Tummy gurgled.

There was no response from Brain – for a very good reason. I had eaten WAY too much ice cream WAY too fast, and we all know what happens when you do that . . .

BRAIN FREEZE!

Chapter Four
FROZEN

The feeling was intense. It started slowly, like the cogs in my mind were winding down, then all of a sudden it got faster and faster. I pulled my head out from under the ice-cream pump, stumbled to my feet and tried to prop myself up in the tight space between the ice-cream machine and the ice-lolly fridge. That's when it really hit me, like a direct snowball strike to the mind. The most unbelievable,

freezing cold,

frosty,

chilly,

crisp,

icy brain freeze I had EVER experienced in my entire life. OK, I know I'm only ten, but, believe me, I've eaten a LOT of ice cream, and on the brain-freeze scale of 0 to 10 this one was **SUB-ZERO**!

'Stay calm,' I told myself. 'It'll be gone in a second.'

But something about this brain freeze was different. It wasn't wearing off like normal. I needed to get out of the cold van. I needed air – the warm summer air!

I clambered out, shivering as I opened the garage doors, and fell on to the grass, waiting for the warm breeze to unfreeze my mind.

That's when I first noticed it – the warm summer breeze. It wasn't there. In fact, the night was suddenly so still it was like there was no air at all.

The next thing I noticed was the sound. There was none. No insects buzzing, no Dad snoring. Nothing.

That's when I knew that something weird was going on – but nothing prepared me for what I saw next.

I scanned the garden. Everything was there, as it had been a few minutes ago – the sprinkler, the insects, the swing under the tree, the flying bat. But nothing was moving.

Everything had frozen.

The bat was hovering mid-flight with its wings spread out wide, just hanging in the air. The spray from the sprinkler fanned overhead, completely motionless, splashing a thousand tiny drops of water, which sparkled in the moonlight like a wave of stars.

The swing under the tree was
completely rigid too, as though
an invisible man was holding it
up, waiting to jump on.

I got to my feet and took a few steps through the motionless garden.

It was like walking into a photograph.

Everything was still.

Everything was calm.

Everything was . . . **FROZEN!**

Suddenly I felt a little **wobbly**. A little **smushy**. As though the frozen cogs of my mind were starting to unfreeze. The world around was swirling slightly, blurring a little, almost melting.

Then, in the flap of a bat's wing, the world came back to life.

The starry sky of spray from the sprinkler splashed down on my head, snapping me back to reality. The bat vanished into the night and the invisible man holding the swing must have jumped on, as it began moving back and forth.

It was my turn to be still for a moment.

'What just happened?' I whispered.

You had a brain freeze so big that you got frozen in time, my brain explained.

'Wow!' I replied.

Let's do it again! rumbled Tummy.

CHAPTER FIVE
RE-FREEZE

I rushed back to Gramps's ice-cream van. Had I really been frozen in time? Could a brain freeze really do that? Could it really work twice?

There was only one way to find out!

I shoved my head back under the pump and pulled the lever, stuffing my face with scrummy vanilla ice cream and overloading my brain with coldness.

I paused and took a breath.

'Here . . . it . . . comes!' I said, preparing myself for the chill.

WHAM!

It hit me a lot quicker this time. Frost seemed to form instantly on the inside of my skull and my thoughts stopped as though they were being squeezed by icy fingers.

'WHOA!' I called out as I felt the world around me slow down.

It was actually happening.

I was becoming frozen in time!

Then suddenly that icy grip released my mind and I found I could relax. I made my way to the front of the van and peered over the seat. In the centre of the dashboard was a little clock. Its hands were completely motionless. I was stuck in this moment.

It had worked.

'YES!' I cheered, and leapt into the

air in celebration, but as I landed I slipped, bashing into the handbrake.

CLICK!

The whole ice-cream van jolted – and, before I could even think, we were on the move!

We rolled backwards, through the open garage doors, leaving an ice-cream-van-shaped cloud of dust behind us where the little grey particles remained frozen in the air like a ghost van.

I started to grab the handbrake, but we shot through the garden, along the driveway and past my house, and I felt the wheels jolt down off the curb and bump on to the quiet, empty road. I was thrown into the back of the van, completely off balance, my brain still slow from the freeze. There was nothing I could do.

Whether I liked it or not, we were rolling backwards down the hill!

I just managed to pull myself up behind the driver's seat as the van zoomed in reverse past our neighbours' houses.

I looked at the round speed dial on the dashboard and saw its little arrow racing up through the thirties, then forties, then . . .

CLUNK!

The door to the glove compartment swung open. Something heavy dropped on to the floor and came sliding to a stop at my slippers.

'An alarm clock?' I croaked.

At my feet was an old mechanical alarm clock, the kind with two large bells on top that looked like they would scare you halfway to crikey if it went off. Its large face looked up at me, and behind its hands I saw smaller dials for the day, month and year. It must have been broken though, as the hands weren't moving and the date was wrong.

Izzy! THE VAN! Brain reminded me.

'Oh, yeah!' I cried, snapping my focus back to the out-of-control vehicle I was in!

Through the windscreen, I saw houses, street lamps and the old crooked post box all swooshing into the distance, but then I suddenly noticed that they weren't just swooshing past – they were changing.

Transforming.

REVERSING!

The Robinson family's front door was repainting itself and the cracked paint now looked shiny and new. The crooked post box un-crooked itself and was as straight as the day it was put in the ground.

Izzy! You're not just travelling backwards down the hill, Brain shouted. *You're travelling back through* **TIME***!*

I gawped outside and saw the days go by, no . . . weeks . . . wait, months, **YEARS**!

'My goodness, Brain – you're right!' I yelled.

I had to stop the van. I forced myself forward and leapt into the driver's seat, but at that precise moment the van went **BUMP** over the speed bump at the bottom of the hill. Now, I know speed bumps are supposed to slow you down, but it turns out that when you're reversing through time speed bumps work in reverse, and we were whooshed along at a chillingly frightening speed. I caught glimpses of blurred houses, which now looked like old-fashioned cottages with thatched roofs. Then they became little wooden shacks, and then they shrank to nothing at all, just empty grassy fields.

The ice-cream van was lurching this way, then that. It bobbed up and down like a boat on water, as though time outside the van was melting, letting us glide through it like a spoon through a tub of soft-scoop raspberry ripple.

It was all so overwhelming. Mesmerizing.

BRINGGGGGG!

An ear-piercing ringing suddenly scared me halfway to crikey! The old alarm clock on the floor had sprung to life and was jiggling about like a startled hamster.

Snapping back to reality, I reached down and pulled as hard as I could on the handbrake. The van screeched and hissed until it finally came to a stop. I scooped up the screaming alarm clock and switched it off before shoving it back in the glove compartment.

There was a sudden eerie silence.

I tried looking through the windscreen, but to my surprise it was completely frosted over. It reminded me of those wintry mornings when I had to wait for Mum and Dad to scrape the ice off the car windows, with the heater on full blast, before we could drive to school.

I went to the door and pulled on the handle. Nothing.

I tried again, but it was as though the door was completely frozen shut!

I sucked in a deep breath, pulled the handle again and barged with all my strength.

CRUNCH!

The door burst open, sending shards of ice flying as I stumbled out into the hot sand.

'Sand?' I gasped.

Where on earth was I?

Or not where, but WHEN?

The sun was blindingly bright.

I blinked until my pupils adjusted.

Then I had to blink some more until my brain had adjusted to the impossible sight in front of me – a humongous, towering pyramid pointing high into the sky!

'Egypt?!' I gasped.

Not just Egypt . . . said Brain.

I looked at the pyramid again but had to squint as the sun reflecting off its brilliant white stones made it hard to see.

'What a second – I've only seen white pyramids in my school book about . . . ANCIENT EGYPT!' I gasped (again!).

Bingo! said Brain proudly.

I suddenly remembered learning how the pyramids were originally covered in white casing stones that shone so brightly in the sunlight that they could be seen on the moon!

A commotion behind me brought me back to the present, which was actually in the past. I turned round to see a familiar sight. **The Great Sphinx of Giza!** The enormous statue with the body of a lion and the head of a human, which had fascinated me in history class. We'd learned all about it and the unsolved riddle of how the huge stone head had lost its nose.

I was snapped out of my daze by angry voices, and I saw a crowd of men waving their arms at me. I couldn't understand what they were saying, but they were pointing at something behind Gramps's ice-cream van.

I quickly ran round to see what it was.

'Oh my . . .' I cried, clasping my hands over my mouth in shock.

Lying on the ground, a little way behind Gramps's ice-cream van, was a giant stone nose!

I looked up at the enormous sphinx as a few little pieces of rubble crumbled off it.

'I am SO sorry!' I said.

Suddenly the robed men stopped what they were doing and dropped to their knees, and I heard another voice behind me.

This time it wasn't a man but a boy, who was wearing a very grand-looking robe and had a fake beard dangling from his chin. He looked about the same age as me, but the surrounding men seemed to tremble in his presence.

The boy shook his head and pulled out a scroll of papyrus.

'Wow! I remember learning about that

in history too!' I said. Papyrus was the first type of paper, made of smushed-up plants. The Egyptians invented it. Super clever!

The boy waved his hand as though he was calling me over.

'Erm . . . hello . . .' I said. 'Sorry about your sphinx's nose!' I pointed to my own nose and mimed breaking it off.

The boy frowned, and something about his expression was suddenly familiar to me. I'd seen his face before . . .

'Oh!' I gasped, suddenly realizing who this boy was. 'You're King Tut . . . I mean, Tutankhamun . . . You're the Pharaoh of Egypt!'

I should have guessed straight away by the fake beard. All pharaohs wore them. Not a clue why though – it looked hot and itchy to me now that I was seeing it in real life.

The young pharaoh, who didn't have the foggiest idea what I was on about, just pointed at the papyrus. I followed his gaze and saw row upon row of amazingly beautiful hieroglyphics – ancient Egyptian writing.

'Sorry,' I said, 'but I can't read – Hang on a sec!'

I had to do a double take. There were lots of beautiful symbols like birds, plants and shapes, but one stood out a mile. It looked like a little blue ice-cream van!

The boy pointed to the van on the papyrus, then at Gramps's van before making a sign with his hands that is universally understood no matter what time you're in.

He was pretending to eat an ice cream!

'Right!' I said, knowing exactly what the young pharaoh wanted.

I quickly jumped into the van, grabbed a

cone and served the most famous pharaoh of ancient Egypt a 99 Flake!

He snatched it out of my hands and began gobbling it up.

'Be careful! If you eat it too fast, you might get a . . . brain freeze!' I warned. Just as those words came out of my mouth I was suddenly very aware that my own brain freeze had completely defrosted in the desert heat. If I was to get back to my own time, I needed to fill my head with ice cream again.

Hooray! Tummy cheered.

'I've got to go! Sorry again about the whole nose thing!' I yelled. I wasted no time and gulped down as much ice cream as I could, as quickly as I could. It was so refreshing after standing in the ancient Egyptian heat, but it went from refreshing to mind-numbingly cold quicker than you can say, *Freezing pharaoh frosticles!*

My head fizzed as though my brain had licked a sour sweet, and I began buckling myself into the driver's seat.

I had no idea how to drive. I'd seen Mum and Dad do it every day, but this wasn't driving through the village to the supermarket. I was trying to drive through time!

There was no time to worry about that though – my brain freeze was kicking in **BIG STYLE**. I turned the key, and the engine chugged into life.

'If reversing took us backwards in time,' I said to myself as I crunched the gear stick until it jammed into first gear, 'then driving forward should take us forward in time.'

Smart! said Brain.

I smiled. 'Thanks.'

I peered out of the window through watery eyes as my brain freeze hit sub-zero again and

I saw the young pharaoh waving goodbye, licking his lips happily before coming to a sudden stop. Little crumbs of sphinx nose hung in mid-air as time froze.

I slammed my foot on the pedal and the ice-cream-van time machine roared into action as I raced forward in time.

CHAPTER SIX
VISITING HOURS

I put my foot down and sped towards home-time, thinking about the adventure I'd just had. I couldn't believe it. How had Tutankhamun known about Gramps's blue ice-cream van? It was almost as though *he'd seen it before*!

I suddenly remembered the silly stories Gramps used to tell me. The ones about escaping from dinosaurs and crashing into pyramids. All of a sudden they didn't seem so silly.

Had Gramps used his ice-cream van to travel through time himself?

That's when the idea hit me.

I could travel through time. I could go to places that used to be, see things that happened long ago, or even *visit people who aren't here any more* . . .

I suddenly knew exactly where I wanted to go.

I was going to visit Gramps!

But how could I get there? I rubbed the frosted window of the ice-cream van with the fluffy sleeve of my cardigan and saw blobby swirls of time and space float past us. How would I know *when* to stop the van?

The glove-compartment door swung open, sending the old mechanical alarm clock crashing to the floor again.

'THAT'S IT!' I cheered. 'I'll set an alarm!'

I grabbed the clock and balanced it on the steering wheel for a closer look, while keeping one eye on the melty-time-wormhole thingy through the frosty windscreen. On the side was a small silver key. It had some teeny-weeny writing engraved on the handle. I squinted and read:

TURN TO SET DATE

I gave it a twist, and the hands on the smaller dial on its face rotated.

Where are we going? asked Brain.

'The question isn't *Where?* – it's *When?*' I explained. 'We're going back to see Gramps.'

Will there be more ice cream? wondered Tummy.

'Definitely!' I smiled as I set the date.

I knew exactly which date I wanted to go to – the first night I visited Gramps in hospital.

How do you know when that was? Tummy asked.

Don't you remember anything? tutted Brain. *It was the day after Valentine's Day.*

'That's right, Brain! I remember all the roses and cards in the hospital.'

And chocolates! added Tummy.

I ignored Tummy and twisted the dial and put my foot down on the accelerator.

The hands on the alarm clock suddenly sprang to life, whizzing round and round.

'It's working!' I cried as the van cruised forward through the warm, melted time outside.

After a few minutes the alarm suddenly exploded with excited ringing.

I slammed both feet on the brake, bringing the van to an abrupt stop.

I switched the alarm off and took a moment to let my head stop spinning before cracking open the door.

Had it worked? Was I really there? The afternoon air ruffled my hair as I stepped out into the familiar car park. I was at the hospital! It was the right place, but was it the right time?

I walked briskly through the hospital towards Gramps's room. Peering into the wards, I saw vases of roses and cards with red hearts on from the day before.

Told you, Brain whispered.

'Shhhhh,' I replied.

I knew the route like the back of my hand.

As I got closer, my heart started pounding

in my chest. If this had worked, I was about to see Gramps again.

But then I realized something – if Gramps was here, then *I* would be too. Not **Now-Me**. I mean **Past-Me**. And if there's one thing I've learned from EVERY time-travel movie EVER made, it's that no good can come of bumping into –

'Hi, Gramps!' Past-Me said from a few metres ahead along the corridor. 'So, this is your new room, is it? Where's the telly?'

I jumped for cover behind a hospital trolley parked in the corridor. I peeped over the top and saw myself from a year ago bounce into Gramps's room carrying a shiny balloon.

'Blue, just like my van!' Gramps replied.

This was weird. **Super weird!** I'd already experienced all this a year ago. Been here, done this! Except that I was over *there* that time, and now I was over *here*, watching over *there* and trying not to let Past-Me *there* see Now-Me *here* . . .

Time travel makes your mind hurt!

'I'll go and get your dinner now,' said the kind voice of Nurse Rita as she left Gramps's room. I put my head down and stared at the floor as she walked past so she couldn't see my face.

Once she was out of sight I crept out from behind the trolley and along to Gramps's room.

'Izzy, my favourite granddaughter!' came his gentle, raspy voice. I was suddenly frozen to the spot but filled with so much warmth at the same time. I was worried for a moment that the effect of his voice might actually melt my brain freeze.

I tiptoed as close as I could and stood just

outside the door, listening to the conversation. *Our* conversation.

'I'm your *only* granddaughter!' Past-Me replied as I mouthed along on the other side of the wall.

'Well, that's true, but I'm sure that even if I had a hundred more, *you* would still be my favourite,' Gramps told Past-Me.

I remembered it all, word for word, as if the lines were permanently frozen in my memory.

Then, right on cue, I heard the squeaky wheel of the dinner trolley coming up the corridor: Nurse Rita was stopping outside each room, delivering food to the other patients. I couldn't wait to see the two ice creams again, and the excitement on Gramps's and Past-Me's faces. I was about to re-experience one of my favourite moments: my first ice cream with Gramps in the hospital!

As Nurse Rita approached Gramps's room, I quickly tucked myself behind a vending machine so that she wouldn't see me as she walked past. The last thing I wanted was Nurse Rita spotting two versions of me in the same place at the same time. Her eyeballs might explode . . . or something like that. Or maybe she'd just do a double take and scratch her head like when she saw the two ice creams – I don't know. Either way, it wasn't worth the risk.

Squeak. Squeak. Squeeeeeeeak!

went the trolley as she stopped one room away from Gramps and took a tray inside. Gramps and Past-Me were next up! While Nurse Rita was gone, I risked a peek round the side of the vending machine . . . and saw something terrible.

On the trolley was Gramps's tray of roast chicken and broccoli.

'Yuck! Looks like tree poop,' joked Gramps, spying the tray from his bed and making Past-Me giggle, but that wasn't the terrible part. The terrible part was the tub of ice cream.

There was only **ONE**!

'That can't be right!' I said to myself. 'There has to be two. There WERE two!'

I remembered it as though it was yesterday. On that very first night Gramps was in the hospital, Nurse Rita had brought in **TWO** ice creams. **TWO!** Gramps had given one to me, and we'd sat and shared stories as we enjoyed them.

My heart started racing. Little drops of ice-cold sweat formed on my forehead. What if we didn't both get an ice cream? What if we didn't get to share stories tonight? It was

THIS night and those TWO ice creams that had started our tradition.

We HAD to get another ice cream!

That's when my brain butted in with a rather genius idea.

You know, you have an ice-cream van full of the stuff, Brain said.

'Great idea, Brain!' I whispered.

I leapt out from my hiding place and sprinted as fast as I could down the slippery hospital corridor. I had to get to the van, pour a tub of ice cream and get it back on the tray before Nurse Rita took it into Gramps and Past-Me.

Now, I'm not sure there's a world record for the fastest ice cream ever poured, but if there was I would totally have made it into the *Guinness Book of Records*. I launched myself into the van, grabbed a little tub from the shelf with one hand, pulled the lever with the other and swirled out the quickest vanilla ice cream in history before legging it back to Gramps.

'Well, enjoy your dinner and I'll be back to collect the tray later,' I heard Nurse Rita say as I skidded round the corner. She was backing out of the room next to Gramps's. I still had time.

I ran, dropped down on my knees and slid the last few metres past the trolley, popping the extra tub of ice cream on to the tray.

YES! Brain said, giving me a mental high-five.

I dashed behind the vending machine again, peeped out and waited.

Squeak. Squeak. Squeeeeeeeak.

'Good evening, Clifford,' Nurse Rita said cheerily as she carried the tray into Gramps's room.

'Evening, young lady,' Gramps said with a twinkle in his eye, making Nurse Rita blush.

'Well, this must be Izzy, your favourite granddaughter! Your granddad has told me all about you.' Nurse Rita smiled at Past-Me, who was beaming from ear to ear at the thought of Gramps telling other people about her.

'Oh!' Nurse Rita said.

This was it. This was the moment!

'What is it, my dear?' Gramps asked, trying to see what Nurse Rita was looking at.

'There are *two* ice creams here!' she said, scratching her head. 'That can't be right. I don't know how that's happened. Everyone gets just one.' She began checking a long list of names and menus and meal times.

'Well, you know, there are two of us,' Gramps said with a little half-smile in Nurse Rita's direction.

She glanced over at Past-Me, who was staring hopefully at the two tubs of vanilla ice cream on the tray.

'Our little secret?' Gramps added with a wink.

Nurse Rita tried to resist, but Gramps always had a way of getting what he wanted. It was those twinkly blue eyes that did it!

'Oh, go on then. But don't tell next door about any extra ice cream or there'll be a riot!' she said.

'What extra ice cream?' Past-Me said with a grin.

'She's certainly your granddaughter, Clifford!' Nurse Rita winked and, with that, she turned and left.

'Cheers to the mysterious extra ice cream!' said Gramps.

'Cheers!' Past-Me replied, raising her tub to meet his.

'Cheers,' I whispered from outside the door.

Chapter Seven
WHAT IF?

I sat listening to Gramps and Past-Me chatting away. I listened to him tell her the story about the time he got shot at by cowboys in the wild west, and the time he was driving through the forest when a gang of men in tights with bows and arrows stole all his ice lollies and gave them to the poor.

As much as I loved sitting there with Past-Me and Gramps, it was getting late and I knew that Past-Me would be leaving soon.

I stood up and carefully took a little peek

round the door frame. There we were. Two happy people with heads full of stories and tummies full of ice cream.

I let out a long sigh and turned away. I didn't want to leave, but it was comforting to think that Past-Me would be back there the next night, doing the exact same thing –

I froze on the spot.

What if the *exact same thing* happened tomorrow? What if Nurse Rita forgot to put two ice creams on the tray again?

I couldn't let that happen.

I broke into a run once more and didn't stop until I was back inside the ice-cream van with my head jammed under the ice-cream machine.

'Must . . . get . . . brain . . . **FREEEEEEZE!**' I winced as the icy frost took hold of my mind. I tumbled forward into the driver's seat, pulled the alarm clock out of the glove compartment and set the alarm for the next day. I turned the key and jammed the gear stick into first with a deafening crunch!

The van lurched forward in time for a second – when the alarm started ringing and I slammed on the brake.

I was in the next day.

I flipped a tub down off the shelf, filled it to the brim with ice cream and ran all the way back into the hospital and up to Gramps's room. Nurse Rita was outside with her trolley.

'Knock, knock!' she said as she peeped inside Gramps's room. 'Are you ready for dinner, Clifford?'

She leaned over slightly, giving me a clear view of the ONE ice cream on the tray!

AHHHHhhhhh!

There was no time, which is ironic for a time traveller. I ran forward, straight past Gramps's room, popping the extra tub on the tray as I zoomed by.

'Oh, look – there's an extra ice cream again!' Past-Me cheered at seeing the two tubs on the tray.

'Well I never . . .' Nurse Rita scratched her head. 'How on earth did that get there?'

I didn't stop running. If this mysterious second ice cream didn't show up two nights in a row, then what was stopping it from not appearing again?

I'd always believed that Nurse Rita was giving us the extra ice cream, and was just pretending not to know where it had come from. But now I wasn't so sure. What if it had been *me* all along? I hadn't always been Now-Me. I had once been sitting in that room. I had once been Past-Me. So, what if it had been Now-Me – or should I say Future-Me – delivering the ice creams each and every night?

I ran back to the magical blue van sitting in the hospital car park. I had a mission. I had a purpose.

'Izzy,' I said to myself as I climbed in. **'You are the Ice-cream Girl!'**

I re-froze time with my brain freeze and drove forward again and again, night after night, time after time, pouring and delivering that extra tub of ice cream for Past-Me on each of the wonderful nights I shared with Gramps in the hospital.

Each time I caught snippets of his amazing stories, his wondrous adventures, now knowing that they were true, all of them. That he really *had* escaped from dinosaurs and crashed into pyramids and done all the things he said he'd done.

I climbed into the van and was about to jam my face under the ice-cream pump when something caught my eye.

A little blinking light on the ice-cream machine.

'Orange?' I whispered.

I knew that red meant empty and green meant full, so I guessed that orange meant it was running low.

I quickly climbed on to the ice-lolly fridge, peered into the top of the ice-cream machine and gasped.

It was nearly empty. Enough ice cream for . . .

'One more trip,' I said, sighing heavily.

I gulped down half of what was left, saving

just enough to fill the last tub, and waited for the wobbly feeling to ease off. Then . . .

WHAM! It hit me.

The final brain freeze.

CHAPTER EIGHT
THE FINAL BRAIN FREEZE

I drove the van forward in time once again until the alarm screamed for me to stop, and I parked it as the sun was starting to set behind the hospital. I filled the last little tub with the last of the swirly vanilla ice cream and jumped out.

As I ran along the corridor towards Gramps's room, I saw Nurse Rita already stepping inside with the dinner tray in her hands.

'Here you go, Clifford. How are you feeling?'

'I'm not . . . too hungry tonight,' he replied.

His voice sounded more croaky than his usual warm tones, and weaker.

'Where's young Izzy tonight?' Nurse Rita asked.

My heart sank. Where *was* Past-Me?

'School concert,' Gramps said with a sigh.

My mouth dropped open. So tonight was **THAT** night. The one night I hadn't come to the hospital.

The night when Gramps had . . .

'Well, that's probably for the best as there's only one ice cream tonight.' Nurse Rita smiled, putting the tray down.

'No there's not!' I said, stepping into the room and revealing the last tub from the van.

'Izzy!' Gramps beamed, propping himself up in his bed. 'You made it!'

'The concert finished early,' I lied. Now, I know it's never right to lie, ESPECIALLY to old people, but that night wasn't any ordinary night.

Gramps smiled at me and patted his hospital bed with his frail hands for me to come and sit next to him. He looked tired, but he still managed to eat his ice cream.

'Any more adventures to tell me about?' I asked.

'Oh, I think I've had all my adventures, Izzy.' He smiled. 'What about you? Do you have any stories to tell me?'

I made myself comfortable and began telling him all about how I'd accidentally broken the nose off the sphinx. He laughed. We both did.

All of a sudden I felt a little drip of ice cream on my hand.

Gramps smiled down at me. 'You'd better eat that before it all melts.'

'Oh no,' I whispered.

'It's OK,' Gramps said to me. 'It's *time*.'

He gave me a little wink and pulled me in for one last hug, like he understood that it was time for me to leave, and I hugged him back, knowing it was time for him too.

I gulped down the ice cream and stayed for just a frozen moment, wishing it would stay frozen forever. But that's the thing about brain freezes – they soon wear off.

I couldn't see through the tears as I hurried back along the corridor to the ice-cream van. I clambered into the driver's seat, started the engine for the last time and drove forward as the frozen world outside seemed to melt around me. The street lamps began flopping over like wilting flowers, and the road ebbed and flowed like a river as I slammed my foot down on the accelerator. Everything started spinning and swirling around the van.

'There it is!' I cried, spotting the inside of our garage through the whirls of time.

We came to a sudden stop – back in the exact same spot in our garage at the end of the garden. Outside, the village clock was chiming midnight and I let out a sigh of relief.

I'd made it. I switched off the ignition and pulled out the keys. It was over.

I opened the door and was about to step out – when suddenly the garage light came on!

Chapter Nine
ME AGAIN!

I froze, not in time but in fear.

Was it Dad? Mum? Had they seen the open door?

'Hello?' I called out. But it wasn't *Now-Me* . . . it was Past-Me, from earlier that night! I recalled how the village clock had struck midnight just as I arrived in the garden, and realized that I must have got back a few minutes before I left. I turned round and saw that the ice-cream van itself looked different. It was exactly as I'd found it earlier that night.

The tubs were re-stocked on the shelf and the little green light on the ice-cream machine was blinking – **FULL!**

I searched my brain for what had happened next and remembered that any second now Past-Me would be yanking the driver's door open and peering inside.

I silently slid over the seat and was about to slip out of the passenger door when I remembered what I had in my hand – **THE KEYS!**

Earlier that night I'd found them dangling in the ignition, ready to go! I quickly stretched across and popped them back in the little keyhole beneath the steering wheel, then dashed out of the passenger door, leaving the keys swinging gently.

As I carefully clicked the door shut, I heard the driver's door **swoosh** open. Past-Me was inside, and I crept back through the garden, into the kitchen and upstairs to bed.

I collapsed in a heap. I was the most exhausted I had ever been in my life, but before I drifted off to sleep my brain whispered:

That was awesome.

Let's do it again tomorrow, rumbled Tummy.

Chapter Ten
THE FUTURE

The school bell **screeched**, making me almost jump out of my skin. The combo of spending the night travelling through time and the warm sunshine flowing through the classroom windows had me on the edge of sleep all afternoon.

I zombied home in a daydream. Had that all actually happened? Had I *really* seen Gramps last night?

Just then my thoughts were interrupted by one of my favourite sounds. The chimes of an ice-cream van.

'Oooh, just what I need,' I said to myself as I headed in the direction of the music. As I turned the corner, I was greeted by the sight of a long queue of children waiting for ice creams outside the shiniest blue ice-cream van I'd ever seen. It looked brand new. Gramps would have loved it. I sighed, and was about to walk away when something caught my eye.

Through a gap in the crowd I saw a very happy young man spinning three ice-cream cones on his fingers while filling them up with wonderful, refreshing ice cream. The crowd cheered as he completed his performance by making three chocolate Flakes appear out of his old-fashioned flat cap, juggling them in the air before catching them, one after the other, in the three separate ice creams.

The children cheered and clapped. I stared.

There was only one man I knew who could make ice creams like that – Gramps! But this man could only have been in his twenties.

'What'll it be?' sang a melodic, husky voice.

I looked around and saw that while I'd been daydreaming the queue had vanished and I was now the only one waiting.

'Oh! Er . . . I . . .'

'Do I know you?' the ice-cream man said, leaning over the counter to get a closer look at me. 'You look very familiar. Have we met in the past?'

As he studied my face, the unmistakable blue of his eyes twinkled magically in the summer sun, making all my doubts melt away.

'No, but I think you might see me again in the future,' I replied with a smile.

THE MIDDLE

Welcome to the mysterious
world under your bed . . .

the magical new tale from bestselling author
TOM FLETCHER

OUT
NOW!

THE
CREAKERS

Illustrated by SHANE DEVRIES

Read on for a taste of
another magical story . . .

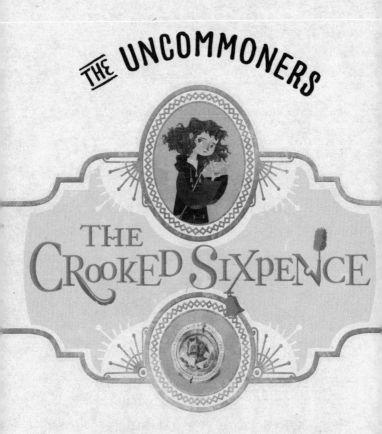

THE UNCOMMONERS

THE CROOKED SIXPENCE

JENNIFER BELL

When Ivy and Seb's grandma is rushed to hospital just before Christmas, neither of them can imagine things getting any worse. But when they return home, they're shocked to discover the house turned upside down, a sinister message scratched on their kitchen wall – and a strange, crooked sixpence, which appears out of thin air. What is it, and who could have done this? But before either of them can wonder, they hear the rumble of voices . . .

Ivy's skin turned to ice. 'What if that's them – the people who did this?'

Seb hurried towards the back door. 'Let's not wait to find out.' He leaped over the remains of a china vase and shot through the patio doors into the garden. Ivy pushed the silver coin into her coat pocket and scrambled after him.

The rain sounded like a snare drum as it hit the flagstones. Ivy tried to keep her balance as she followed Seb round the corner and into the alley between the house and a neighbouring field. She wiped her eyes clumsily, completely forgetting that she had a hood.

'Ivy, watch it!' Seb called.

She ground to a stop, arms flailing. Beside the toe of her wellington boot was a large brown hessian sack, the soil spilling out of it. *Granma Sylvie's potatoes.* Ivy winced. She'd grown them in that sack for ever. 'Sorry,' she whispered.

Carefully she hopped over it and inched towards Seb, who was crouching down next to the garage at the front of the house. The rain chimed off its corrugated-iron roof, masking the sound of her footsteps. She tucked herself behind a section of dense yew hedge and angled her head till she could see. Her jaw dropped.

What the—?

In Granma Sylvie's drive stood a funeral coach, complete with four black horses. It was long and rectangular, with glass sides and a strip of ornate carving along the top. Every inch had been lacquered with ebony gloss which matched the head-feathers of the horses. Ivy had seen something like it only once before, on the way to school. Her mum had slowed to let it pass. *That* coach had been carrying a coffin. This one was empty.

No . . . wait.

Ivy squinted. It wasn't empty. Inside she could see a boy. His image was made fuzzy by the rain, but he had dark hair and cinnamon-brown skin. He was sitting with his knees up and his hands clasped around them, his head bent so Ivy couldn't see his face.

'Seb!' she hissed, but his gaze was fixed elsewhere: on Granma Sylvie's doorstep. Ivy turned to see what was going on.

Standing beneath the porch were two men in matching black uniforms: a balding, red-faced fellow with a huge belly and, beside him, a tall lean figure with slicked-back hair, chalky skin and dark glasses. Both men wore ankle-length cloaks, gloves with gleaming silver studs across the knuckles and hats shaped like a pirate's tricorne.

'Shall I use this now, sir?' the red-faced man asked. 'Try to flush out anyone who might still be here?' In his hand was a large conch shell – one of the spiky, salt-encrusted ones you found on rocky beaches. When the other man didn't reply, he said, 'Officer Smokehart, sir?'

The tall man turned towards him slowly, his chin raised. 'Lower the shell,' he said. His voice sent chills shooting down the back of Ivy's neck. It sounded like a knife – vicious and cold. 'If there's anyone inside, we don't want to give them time to escape. They might reveal something useful under questioning.'

Ivy shivered. There was something about Officer Smokehart that wasn't quite natural. Maybe it was the way he was standing: straight-backed and still, like a robot.

'Just imagine, Constable,' he breathed, steepling his thin fingers, 'what answers might lie behind this door; what dark revelations we might find festering in the shadows. For over forty years we've lived without knowing the truth of what happened that night.'

'Twelfth Night,' the constable said, a little uncertainly, setting the conch down on the ground.

Smokehart gritted his teeth. 'Yes, of course

Twelfth Night. It is the greatest unexplained mystery of the modern era. The entire Wrench family – a mother, father daughter and three brothers – disappear on one fateful night. We don't know why they vanished, or how. We don't even know what role they played during the Great Battle . . . until now.' His thin lips curled into a smile. 'The quartermasters will have no choice but to promote me for this, mark my words.'

The constable gulped and stood to attention. He looked at the broken lock. 'Looks like we're not the first ones here, though, sir.'

Officer Smokehart peered down through his dark glasses. Ivy wondered why he was wearing them – it wasn't as if it was sunny.

'She has many enemies,' he said, considering. 'It's possible that one of them has got to her before us. Arm yourself.'

The constable nodded quickly, swept back his cloak and pulled out . . .

Ivy squinted. Surely she was seeing this wrong. The rain was distorting her vision; it must be. White plastic. Long handle. Rounded head of bristles.

No, it was a *toilet brush*. As Smokehart drew an identical one from the loop on his belt, Ivy noticed something else. The bristles were moving slightly. If she concentrated hard enough through the drumming of the rain, she could hear them crackling. And what was that jumping from the end . . . *sparks*?

Ivy's legs started to tremble.

From his crouched position, Seb waved at her furiously, his nostrils flaring. He signalled towards the far gate, where their bikes were leaning against the fence.

Ivy nodded down the road towards Bletchy Scrubb. That's where they needed to go.

'Don't think we should spend long here, sir,' the constable commented, pushing open the front door. 'We've got that young tea-leaf in the carriage – needs to be taken back to Lundinor for processing.'

Smokehart raised pencil-thin eyebrows above his dark glasses. 'Not long? Constable, if this really is where Sylvie Wrench has been hiding for forty years, then we will stay *as long as is necessary* to uncover whatever evidence may be inside.' Holding his toilet brush aloft, he marched over the threshold into the hallway beyond. The constable followed.

The name *Sylvie Wrench* was ringing in Ivy's ears as she saw Seb getting to his feet. *Sylvie* . . .

She walked slowly, as if in a dream.

Granma . . .

'Ivy,' Seb mouthed. 'Bikes.'

She snapped back to reality and followed Seb across the gravel to collect her bike. Her wet hands trembled as she tugged her hood back and fumbled with the strap of her helmet. *Sylvie Wrench* . . . *Twelfth Night* . . . Her head was spinning. She got onto her bike and put her foot on the pedal.

And then a voice like thunder filled the air: '*This is Officer Smokehart of the First Cohort of Lundinor Underguard! You are breaking GUT law. Remain where you are, by command of the Four Quartermasters of Lundinor!*'

*

Ivy shrieked, 'Seb, go!' She slung Granma Sylvie's bag across her back before kicking away from the ground. Up ahead, Seb's wheels squealed as he shot onto the tarmac and skidded round a corner.

Ivy flashed a look over her shoulder, pedalling frantically. Officer Smokehart was in Granma Sylvie's porch, holding the conch shell to his lips. The constable had already climbed aboard the black coach.

Rising up off the saddle, Ivy pushed down on the pedals as hard as she could. What sounded like a hailstorm started up behind her, drawing closer.

The horses . . . !

The coach was on the road.

'Stay close to me,' Seb shouted. 'This way!' He turned off the road, darting through a small gap in the hedgerow and heading into a field. 'They're too big to come after us,' he yelled. 'They'll have to go the long way round.'

Ivy could see what he was planning. Ahead of them, the road curved round the edge of the field. Seb was cycling straight across the grass towards an open gate on the opposite side. If they were lucky, they'd get there before the coach.

Ivy hurtled after him. Her bike squeaked and groaned over the bumpy ground. Glancing back, she could see the top of the coach above the hedgerow – it was gaining on them now. The constable was craning forward, flicking a whip through the air, while the horses' head-feathers tossed around madly.

'They're catching up!' Ivy warned. She didn't know how much longer she and Seb could stay in front.

'Go faster,' he yelled at her, his cheeks bright red, his legs a blur. 'We have to make it!'

Ivy surged forward into the battering rain. Seb was only metres away from the gate.

'Ivy!' he shouted, crossing the road.

She looked back at the coach, which was nearly upon them. She caught a glimpse of the dark-haired boy inside, pushing against the glass, steadying himself against the jolts.

Smokehart's voice filled the air again. '*STOP WHERE YOU ARE!*'

Ivy faltered as she reached the road. The horses were metres away. She stared helplessly at Seb. His eyes were wide. She screamed his name, and then . . .

The carriage was between them.

A splintering, creaking noise split the air. The constable howled. Ivy was thrown head first off her bike; her helmet took the worst of the impact as she thudded into the hard earth beside the road. Granma Sylvie's bag crunched painfully against her ribs and cold mud splashed onto her cheeks.

When she opened her eyes, she saw a face: angled cheekbones, dark-chocolate eyes, skin like polished teak.

It was the boy from the coach.

'You all right?' he asked. The rain had soaked his long, straggly hair and was running down onto his shoulders.

'Uh . . .' Ivy murmured. Her brain felt like it was made of marshmallow. She struggled with the strap of her helmet and eventually tugged it off. 'What happened?'

'Underguards,' the boy grunted. 'Must have been too interested in chasing you to notice the ice on the road.'

Ivy raised a shaky hand to her temple. *Underguards . . . ?*

'They've overturned in the next field,' the boy continued. 'Looks like your friend saw it just in time.'

Friend? The fog in Ivy's head started to clear. Her neck prickled as she remembered: *Seb.* Carefully she lifted herself up. Her bike was lying some five metres away, the wheels trilling as they spun. A familiar figure was staggering across the grass.

'Ivy!' Seb called breathlessly. 'Are you OK?'

She tried to get to her feet. The boy helped her up. His skinny figure, slim-fitting jeans, black leather jacket and red high-top basketball shoes reminded her of the lead singer in The Ripz. 'Easy,' he said. 'You're gonna feel like you've just had a sack of flour dumped on your head, but just try to breathe. Everything moving?'

Slowly, systematically, she wiggled her fingers and toes and tilted her head from side to side. She suspected there were probably a few cuts and grazes hiding beneath her coat but she wouldn't need an ambulance. 'I think so. Seb?' She focused on him as he approached. His gaze was fixed on the stranger in front of him.

'Who are you?' Seb asked. Now that they were next to each other, Ivy could see they were probably of a similar age. 'Are you one of them?'

The boy arched an eyebrow. 'One of the Ugs? Hell no. I'd rather be a ghoul.' His eyes went nervously to a spot by Ivy's feet. 'I've had my fair share of running from them, though – if you two want to get away, you don't have much time.'

Ivy glanced down, wondering what he was looking at. Standing in the grass by her feet was a small leather suitcase with brass latches. A brown paper tag was tied around the handle. *Strange* . . . Ivy hadn't glimpsed it in the field earlier.

She bent over and gripped the handle. 'How did this get—?' The question caught in her mouth as a wave of tingly heat spread through her fingers. She gave a short gasp: the suitcase felt so much like a hot potato, she struggled not to drop it. She'd had this sensation before, when she held the silver coin. The only difference was that touching the suitcase felt more intense.

The boy stiffened and threw a gloved hand towards the case. 'That's mine.'

Ivy held it out to him. 'All right, I was just—'

Just then, she heard the rattle of a harness in the road.

'The underguards,' the boy hissed. 'There's no time . . .' He snatched the case, unfastened the latches, opened it on the grass and dropped onto his knees beside it. 'Are you coming?'

Ivy's head was spinning. 'Coming where?'

Seb dug his fingers into her shoulder. 'Ivy, we need to do something – now!'

Too late.

The rapid fire of hoofbeats sounded on the other side of the hedgerow. A wild neigh followed the clatter of something loud and heavy, and then Officer Smokehart came tearing along towards them. He moved impossibly fast, his arms pumping as his black cloak mushroomed up behind him. Ivy noticed with a jolt that his face and neck were no longer smooth and pale; they were covered with tiny scarlet dots, like drops of blood. In his outstretched hand he waved his toilet brush, the bristles alive with blue sparks.

'Go – *now*!' The boy yanked on Ivy's arm, hauling her to the ground.

She felt wet grass under her hands as something pushed down on the back of her head. She saw the brown suede lining of the suitcase expanding before a cold feeling slipped down her spine and she was swallowed by darkness.

WORLD
**BOOK
DAY**

Hello

We hope you enjoyed this book.

Proudly brought to you by **WORLD BOOK DAY**,

the **BIGGEST CELEBRATION** of the **magic** and **fun** of **storytelling**.

We are the **bringer of books to readers** everywhere

and a **charity** on a **MISSION**

to take you on a **READING JOURNEY**.

EXPLORE
new worlds
(and bookshops!)

EXPAND
your
imagination

DISCOVER
some of the very
best authors and
illustrators with us.

A **LOVE OF READING** is one of life's greatest gifts.

And this book is **OUR gift to YOU**.

HAPPY READING.
HAPPY WORLD BOOK DAY!

WORLD BOOK DAY

SHARE A STORY

Discover and share stories from breakfast to bedtime.

THREE ways to continue **YOUR** reading adventure

1 VISIT YOUR LOCAL BOOKSHOP

Your go-to destination for awesome reading recommendations and events with your favourite authors and illustrators.

FIND YOUR LOCAL BOOKSHOP
booksellers.org.uk/ bookshopsearch

2 JOIN YOUR LOCAL LIBRARY

Browse and borrow from a huge selection of books, get expert ideas of what to read next and take part in wonderful family reading activities – all for FREE!

FIND YOUR LOCAL LIBRARY
findmylibrary.co.uk

3 GO ONLINE AT WORLDBOOKDAY.COM

Fun podcasts, activities, games, videos, downloads, competitions, new books galore and all the latest book news.

Illustrations © Jim Field

SPONSORED BY

NATIONAL **BOOK** tokens

Celebrate stories. Love reading.